To Christien and Caylin, who keep me young at heart.
—W. S.

To all the children I visit at schools that
make drawing Turkey so much fun!
—L. H.

two lions

Text copyright © 2019 by Wendi Silvano
Illustrations copyright © 2019 by Lee Harper
All rights reserved.

Published by Two Lions, New York
www.apub.com
Amazon, the Amazon logo, and Two Lions are trademarks of Amazon.com, Inc., or its affiliates.

ISBN-13: 9781542040372
ISBN-10: 154204037X

The illustrations are rendered in watercolor and pencil on Arches hot press watercolor paper.
Book design by Tanya Ross-Hughes
Printed in China
First Edition
10 9 8 7 6 5 4 3 2 1

Turkey's Eggcellent Easter

by
Wendi Silvano

illustrated by
Lee Harper

The sun was bright. The air was fresh.
It was a perfect spring morning.
Turkey read the sign one more time.

Easter Egg Hunt
Saturday morning at 9:00 a.m.

Find one of the "special" eggs
to win an *eggstraspecial* prize!

"This is gobble, gobble great!" said Turkey.
"I wonder what the *eggstraspecial* prize is."

"I heard something about chocolate and jelly beans," said Cow.

"Y-y-yum!" whinnied Horse. "We've got to get one of those eggs!"

"But animals aren't allowed at the egg hunt," grunted Pig. "It's just for kids."

"If they don't know we're there, we won't get the boot . . . ," said Sheep.

"Turkey," said Cow. "You go in disguise and snoop out one of those eggs. We'll stay camouflaged and be your backup."

"How *eggciting!*" crowed Rooster. "A secret mission!"

"Gobbledy good idea!" Turkey said. "I'll be a rabbit. No one will notice an extra rabbit hopping around."

The day of the egg hunt arrived.

And Turkey's costume wasn't bad.
In fact, he looked just like a rabbit . . . almost.

He kept a sharp eye as he hopped around and around the park.

Finally he spotted a special egg behind a rock.

"Target straight ahead six hops," he whispered to Cow.

"*Moove* in," whispered Cow.

"Copy that," said Turkey.

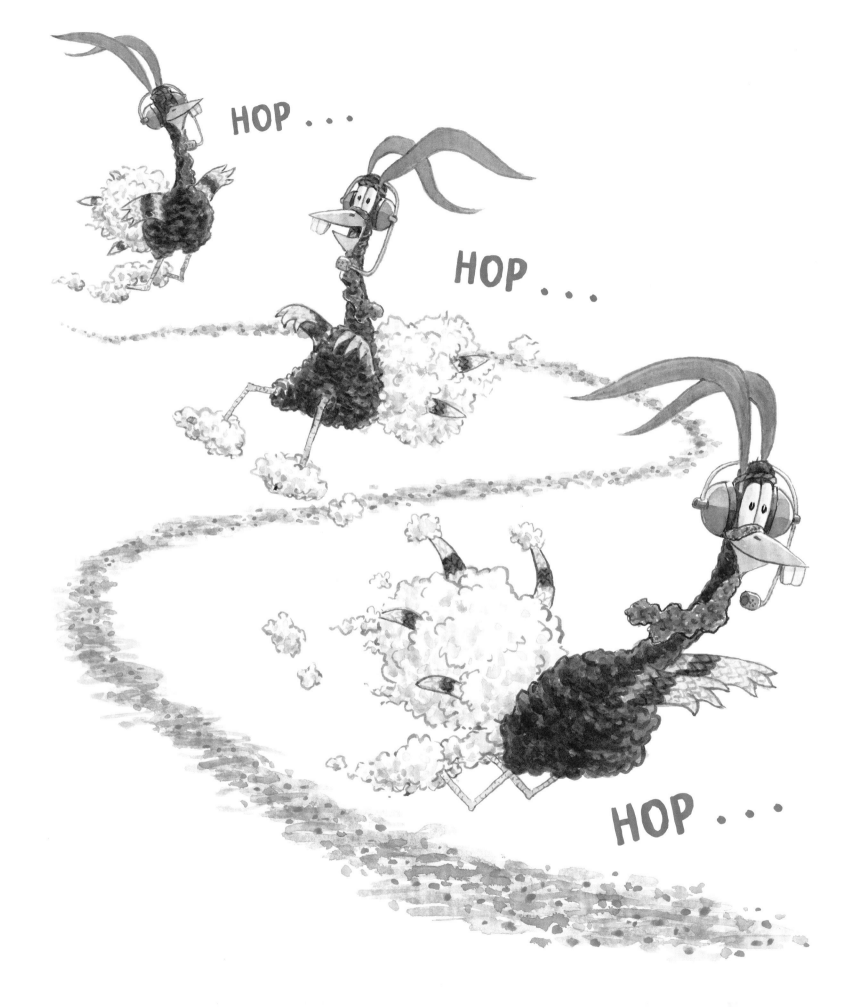

"Alert! Alert!
Child approaching!"
whispered Cow.

Turkey froze.

"Some *bunny's* in big trouble," said the child.
"This egg hunt is for kids. Hop on out of here!"

"Oh, gobble, gobble," grumbled Turkey.

"Pssst . . . time for a new disguise, Turkey," said Pig.

Turkey looked around. "I know *eggsactly* what to do."

His costume wasn't bad. In fact, Turkey looked just like a daffodil . . . almost.

"Pssst . . . ," whispered Horse. "I think I spy a special egg over by the bench."

"Copy that," said Turkey.

He carefully inched his way over and planted
himself next to the bench.

There it was.

Turkey leaned and reached out
to grab the egg.

Mable Mayberry glanced down.
"Oh, what an *eggstremely* beautiful flower!
I think I will take it home for my Easter bouquet."

"Abort! Abort!" whispered Sheep.
Turkey bolted just before he got plucked.

"Gobble, gobble . . . thwarted again!" groaned Turkey.
"I've got to find one of the special eggs before they're all gone."

"Psst . . . ," whispered Rooster. "I spy a special egg up on top of the slide.
We've got to get you up there undetected."

"Copy that," said Turkey. "I think I have an idea."

His costume wasn't bad. In fact, Turkey looked just like a bumblebee . . . almost.

"Ready?" asked Horse.

"I gobble, gobble guess," said Turkey. "Fire away!"

Turkey sailed through the air.

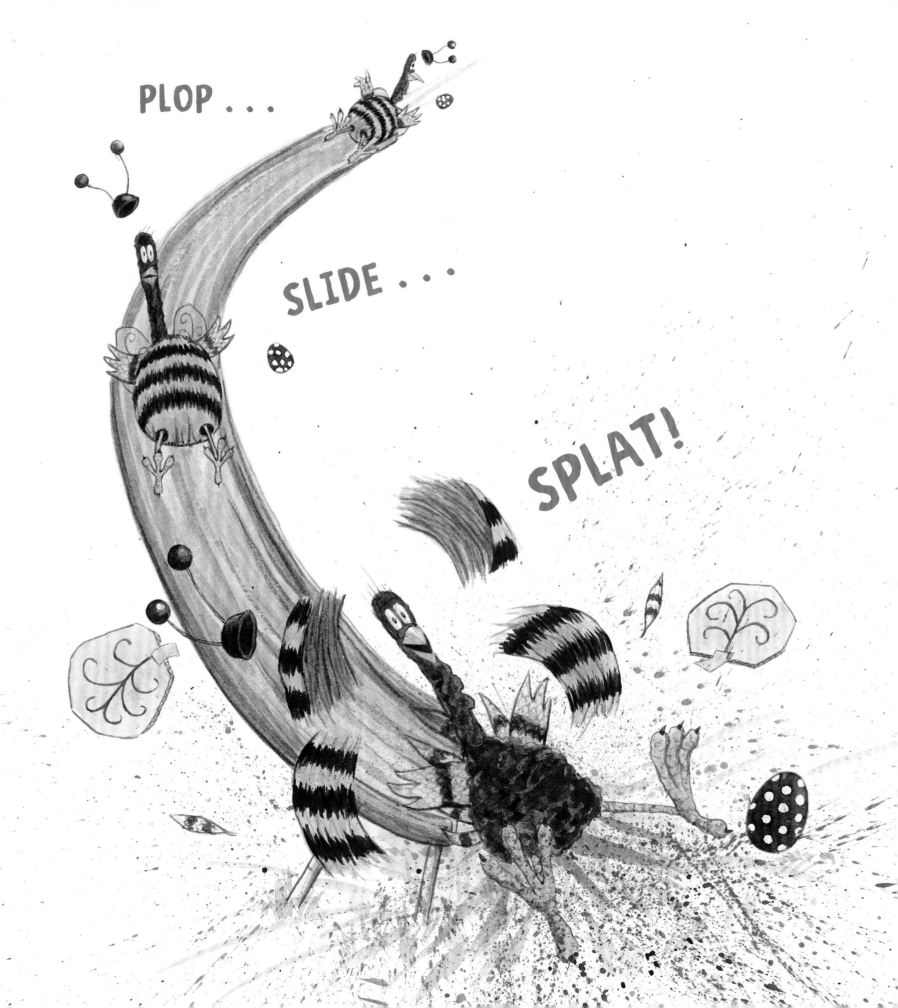

"Some*sting*'s not right here," scolded Farmer Jake.
"No turkeys allowed at the egg hunt!
Buzz your way back to the barn!"

"Oh, gobble, gobble, gobble," moaned Turkey.
"Our mission has been sabotaged at every turn."

"I'm no *eggspert*," said Rooster.
"But maybe to get a special egg you have to be one."

"*Eggcellent* idea!" said Turkey. All the animals agreed.
His costume wasn't bad. In fact, Turkey looked just like a special egg . . . almost.

"On your mark!" crowed Rooster. "Get set! ROLL!"

Turkey was rolled from Cow . . .

to Horse . . .

to Pig . . .

to Sheep . . .

. . . to the middle of the action.

But before he could look around for a special egg, he was nabbed.
"I found one!" cried Max. "I found a giant special egg!"

At the prize table Max turned in his "special" egg. Farmer Jake and Edna looked at Turkey. Then they looked at each other . . . and laughed . . . and laughed. "This is truly an *eggstraspecial* egg," Farmer Jake said to Max. "I think maybe you—and your egg—can each choose a prize."

And they did.

"Mission accomplished!" said Turkey.
"What an eggcellent Easter!"